THIS BOOK IS DEDICATED TO MY WONDERFUL WIFE, LUCY, WHOSE BRILLIANT IDEA IT WAS, AND WHO'S BEEN WAITING, SOMEWHAT PATIENTLY, FOR OVER TWENTY YEARS FOR ME TO DO A CHILDREN'S BOOK! I HOPE THIS IS JUST THE FIRST OF MANY. I'D ALSO LIKE TO THANK MY WHOLE FAMILY FOR THEIR CONSTANT LOVING SUPPORT AND HELP, AND ALSO THE EMMAUS PUBLIC LIBRARY STAFF FOR THEIR ENTHUSIASTIC ENCOURAGEMENT. SPECIAL THANKS TO LISA DUGAN FOR HER INVALUABLE ASSISTANCE CONNECTING ME WITH HARPERCOLLINS, AND TO MARGARET, MY SUPEREDITOR.

SuperHero ABC
Copyright © 2006 by Bob McLeod
Manufactured in China.

Library of Congress Cataloging-in-Publication Data
McLeod, Bob.   SuperHero ABC / by Bob McLeod. — 1st ed.   p.   cm.   Summary: Humorous SuperHeroes such as Goo Girl and The Volcano represent the letters of the alphabet from A to Z.   ISBN 978-0-06-074514-1 (trade bdg.) — ISBN 978-0-06-074515-8 (lib. bdg.) — ISBN 978-0-06-074516-5 (pbk.)
[1. Heroes—Fiction. 2. Alphabet.]   I. Title.   PZ7.M478716Su 2006   2004022180   [E]—dc22   CIP   AC

Typography by Meredith Pratt
15 16 17 SCP 20 19 18 17 16 15
❖
First Edition

# Mm

HE WEARS A MASK!